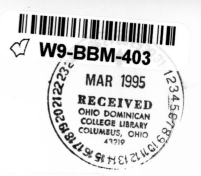

for Julia

She shall lean her ear
In many a secret place
Where rivulets dance their wayward round,
And beauty born of murmuring sound
Shall pass into her face.

William Wordsworth

THE
OLD STUMP

STORY AND PICTURES BY

JOHN HAWKINSON

ALBERT WHITMAN & Company • Chicago

© 1965 Albert Whitman & Company. L. C. Catalog Card 65-23883
Published simultaneously in Canada by George J. McLeod, Ltd., Toronto. Printed in U.S.A.

Once upon a time
in the middle of
A GREAT BIG FOREST

in an old, old stump
there lived a tiny little
mouse.

He had two
BROTHERS,

THREE SISTERS,

and a BIG FAT
MAMA.

Right in here is where he lived.

136435

At night when the moon
shone through the forest
the little mouse and his
two brothers and his three
sisters would come out and
play on the old, old stump,

and the
BIG FAT
MAMA MOUSE
would stay inside
and clean up
the nest.

In the morning when the sun
came up and shone through the forest

the little mouse

and his
two brothers

and his
three sisters

would stop their playing
and return to the nest.

Then they would all
snuggle up and go to sleep.

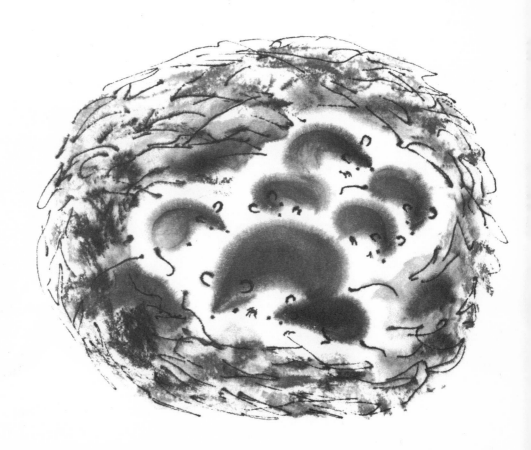

The dew on the moss
that grew on the stump
sparkled in the morning sun.

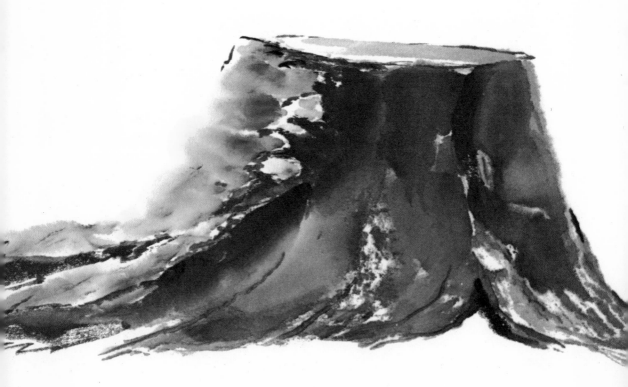

A wood thrush
darted
through
the trees.

He perched
on the stump
and sang his
song of silver
bells.

In the nest below
Mama Mouse opened
one eye and listened.

But the little mouse
slept on without
hearing a note,

and his two brothers
and his three sisters
slept through the song.

Two chipmunks popped out of a hole
in the ground and scampered
through the leaves.

They climbed on the stump
and chased each other
around and around.

The little mouse
woke up and
saw his mother
fast asleep
so he closed
his eyes again.

A butterfly
came to rest
its wings and
bask in the
sun that shone
on the stump.
Then it flew
away without
making a sound.

Through the woods
came a group of
boys, their laughter
causing the birds
to fly.
"Look, look, there is
a stump! Let's climb it
and see how far
we can jump,"
the boys cried.

The ground shook and there
were shrieks and yells.
The little mouse and his
brothers and sisters all
woke up with a start and
went squeaking and running
around the nest in terror.

Mama Mouse
shushed
her children
as they
clung to her.

The boys
went away
and a blue jay
came down
to sharpen
his bill
on the stump.

This didn't wake the mice.

A fat old toad came and sat
in the shadow of the stump and
patiently waited for flies.
And the mice slept on.

A grouse came strutting
through the woods, stopping
here and there to peck.
He flew up on the stump
to beat his wings —
BOOM, BOOM, BOOM!
They made a noise heard
far, far away
for a lady grouse to hear.

The little mouse stirred
in the nest, but
he did not open
his eyes.

As the sun was
about to go down
a porcupine came by
and climbed to the
top of the stump.

"My, goodness, what
a short tree," and
"Sniff, sniff, there's
nothing here to eat.
Oh, well, I'll take
a little snooze,"
he thought.

And the old sun finally went down and
the moon came up and shone like silver
on the old stump and the sleepy porcupine.

The little mouse
was the first one
out to play. He
ran to the top
of the stump
and BUMPED
right into the
sleepy porcupine.

The little mouse
squeaked in surprise
and scampered
right back to
the nest and his
big fat mama.

An evening breeze
blew the scent of
aspen trees to the
porcupine and he
sniffed and stirred
in his sleep.
Another breeze blew,
and he woke up and
slowly ambled away.

The little mouse peeked out and saw
that the porcupine had gone away.
Soon his two brothers and three sisters
followed him up to the top of the
old stump, and they all played in the
moonlight until the sun came up again.